DATE DUE

JUL 2

ZIG
AND
WIKKI

IN
SOMETHING ATE
MY HOMEWORK

NADJA SPIEGELMAN & TRADE LOEFFLER

ZIG AND WIKKI

IN

SOMETHING ATE MY HOMEWORK

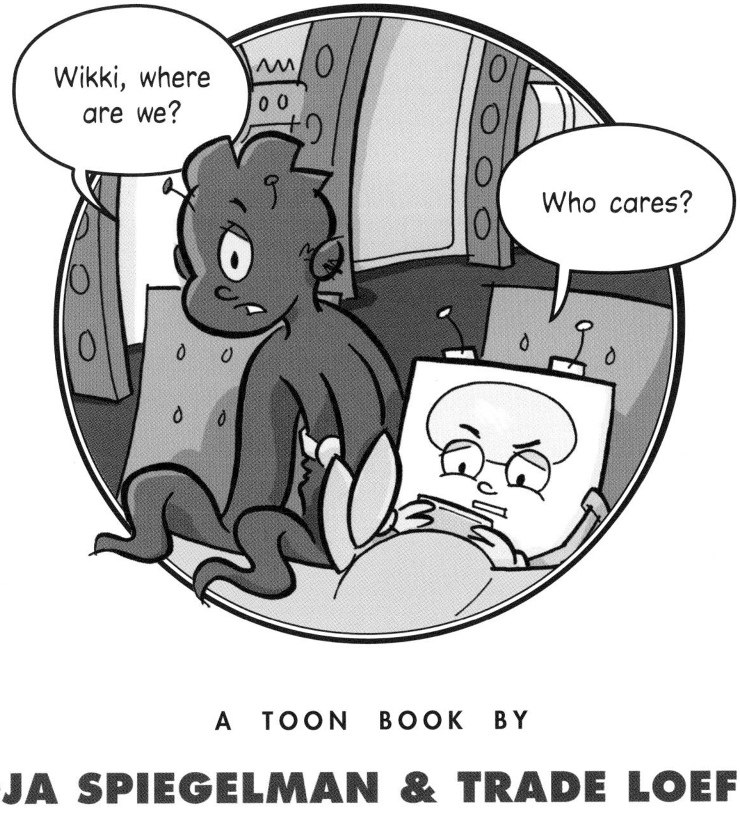
Wikki, where are we?
Who cares?

A TOON BOOK BY

NADJA SPIEGELMAN & TRADE LOEFFLER

TOON BOOKS, A DIVISION OF RAW JUNIOR, LLC, NEW YORK

Visit us at www.abdopublishing.com

Reinforced library bound editions published in 2014 by Spotlight, a division of the ABDO Group, PO Box 398166, Minneapolis, MN 55439. Spotlight produces high-quality reinforced library bound editions for schools and libraries. Published by agreement with Raw Junior, LLC. All rights reserved.

Printed in the United States of America, North Mankato, Minnesota.
042013
092013
♻ This book contains at least 10% recycled material.

For my mother -*Nadja*
For Mohammad Riza -*Trade*

Editorial Director: FRANÇOISE MOULY
Advisor: ART SPIEGELMAN

Book Design: FRANÇOISE MOULY & JONATHAN BENNETT

Guest Editor: GEOFFREY HAYES
Guest Nature Researcher: JUDY FUNK

All photos used by permission, all rights reserved. Page 13: © Mailthepic / Dreamstime.com; Page 14: © 2008 Terrence Jacobs; Page 18: © Le Do / Dreamstime.com; Page 21: © Clearviewstock / Dreamstime.com; Page 22: © 2007 Maianna Fitzgerald; Page 30: © 2009 Lyn Chesna; Page 40: Fly larva © 2009 Luis Buján, Dragonfly © Tanya Puntti (*tanya-ann.com*), Frog © Alptraum / Dreamstime.com, Raccoon © Eric Isselée / Dreamstime.com. BACKCOVER: Frog © Shao Weiwei / Dreamstime.com.

Library of Congress Cataloging-in-Publication Data
This book was previously cataloged with the following information:

Spiegelman, Nadja.
Zig and Wikki in Something ate my homework : a Toon book / by Nadja Spiegelman & Trade Loeffler.
  p. cm. -- (TOON Books)
Summary: Zig and Wikki arrive on earth to search for a pet for Zig's class assignment.
[1. Graphic novels. 2. Pets --Fiction. 3. Science fiction.]
PZ7.7.S65 Zi 2010
[Fic]

2009028017

ISBN 978-1-61479-157-7 (reinforced library bound edition)

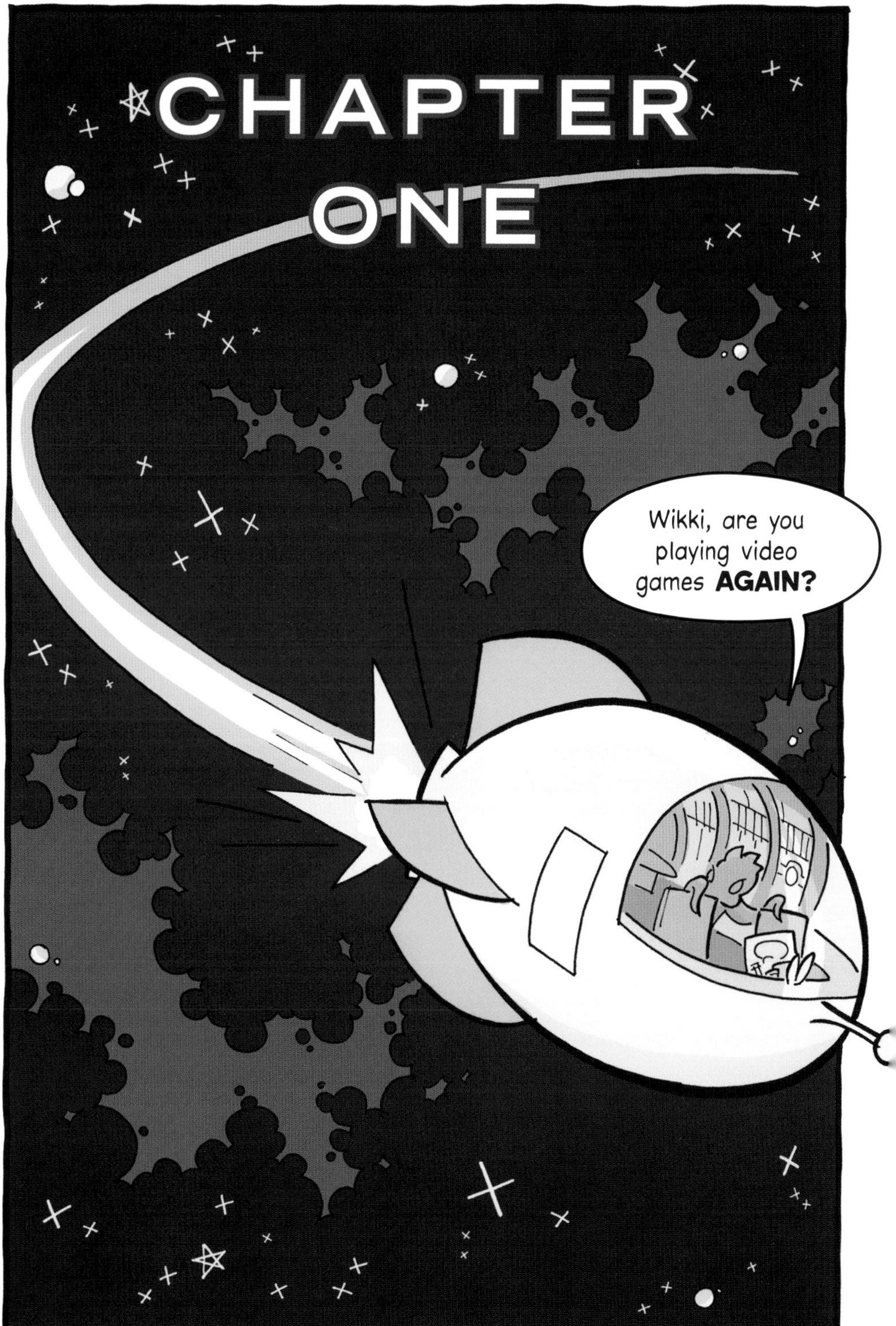
CHAPTER ONE
Wikki, are you playing video games **AGAIN?**

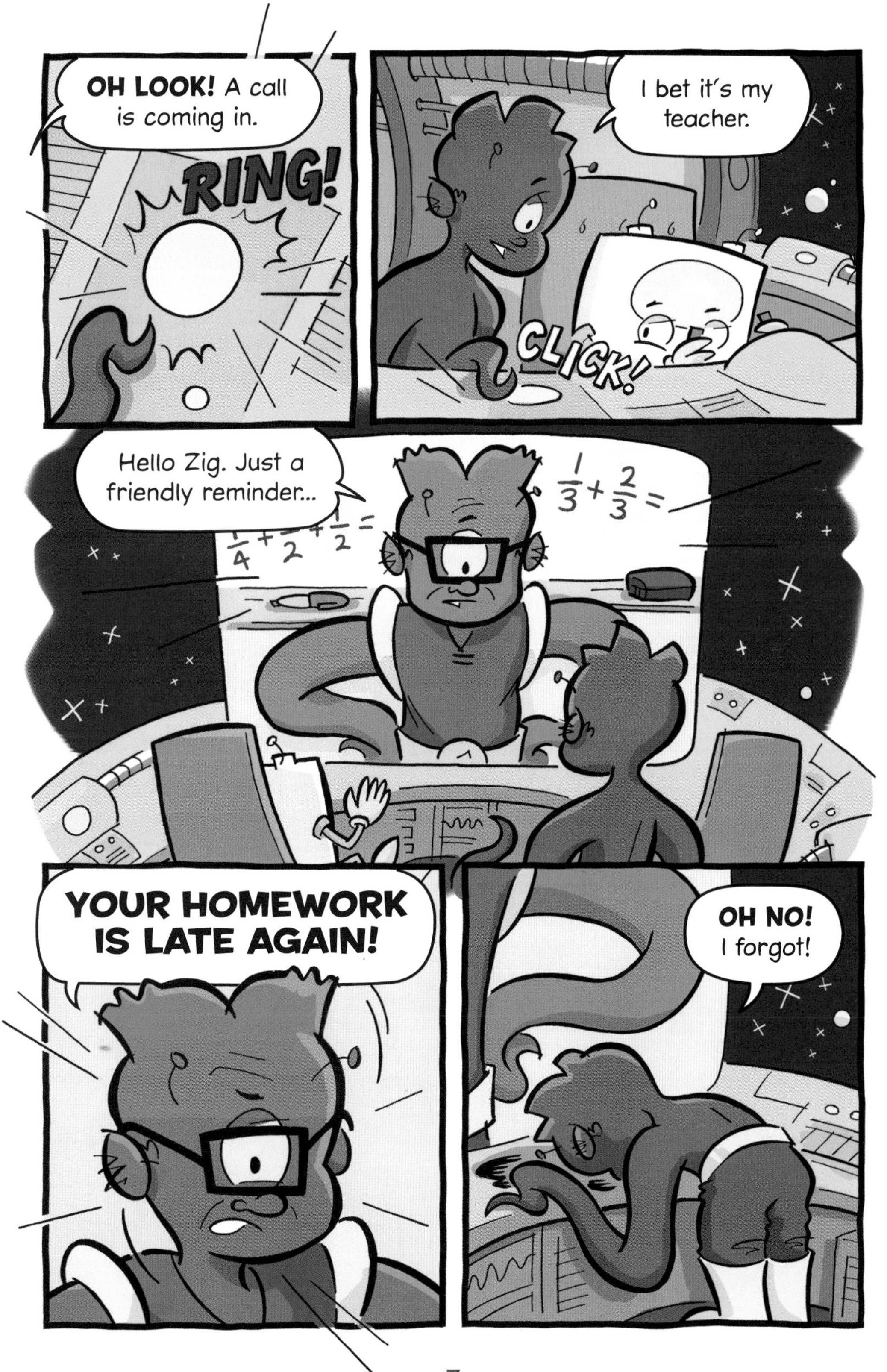
OH LOOK! A call is coming in.
RING!
I bet it's my teacher.
CLICK!
Hello Zig. Just a friendly reminder...
1/3 + 2/3 =
YOUR HOMEWORK IS LATE AGAIN!
OH NO! I forgot!

EVERYONE else got a pet for the class zoo but you!

EEK

ROOPY

ZIG

SPLAZ

CLARK

CLASS PETS

If you don't bring in a pet today...

...I'M CALLING YOUR PARENTS!

AZ

Oh, and one more thing...

You and Wikki always get into trouble when you're together...

...so do this on your own!

CLICK!

8

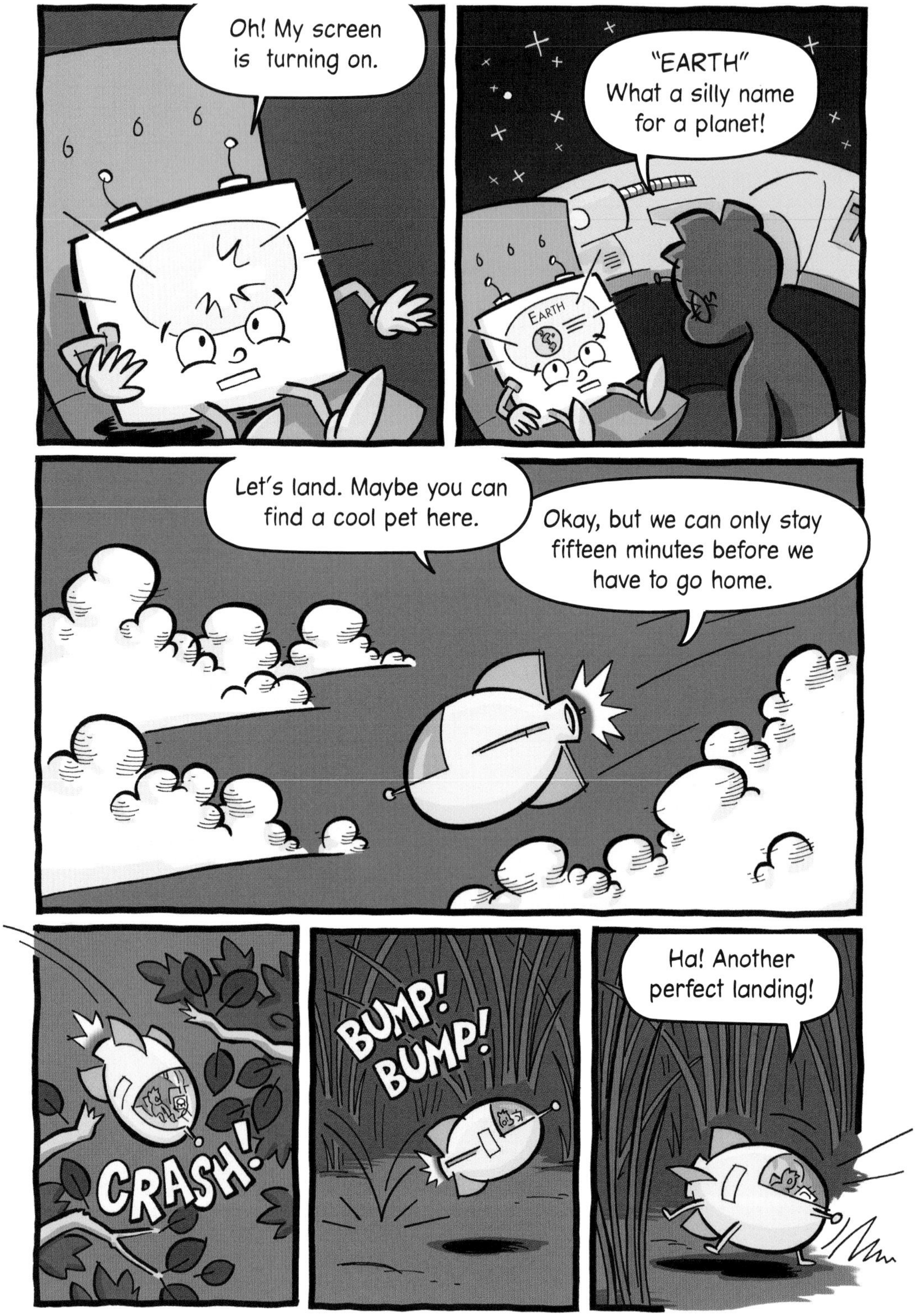
Oh! My screen is turning on.
"EARTH" What a silly name for a planet!
EARTH
Let's land. Maybe you can find a cool pet here.
Okay, but we can only stay fifteen minutes before we have to go home.
CRASH!
BUMP! BUMP!
Ha! Another perfect landing!

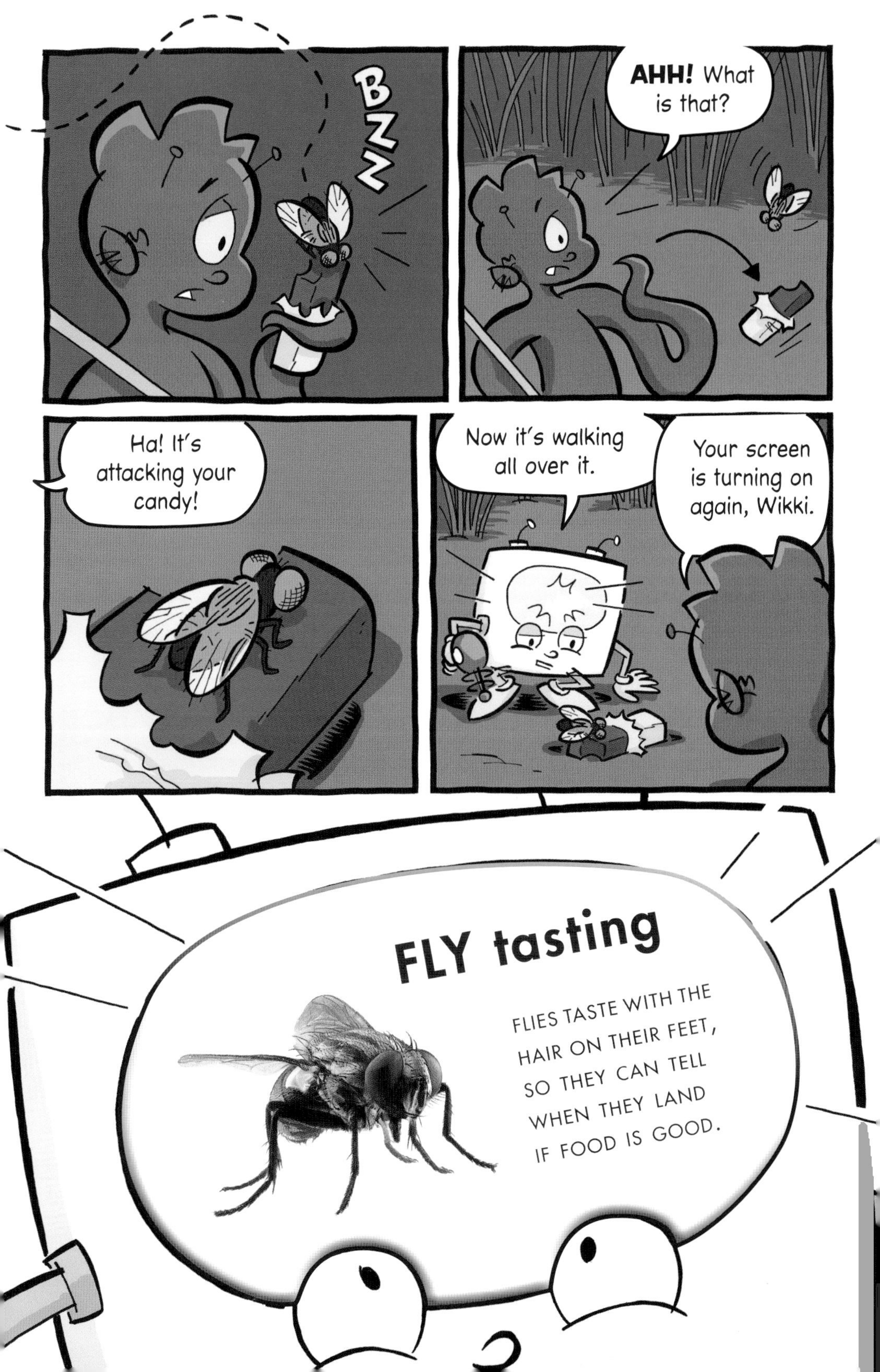
BZZ
AHH! What is that?
Ha! It's attacking your candy!
Now it's walking all over it.
Your screen is turning on again, Wikki.
FLY tasting
FLIES TASTE WITH THE HAIR ON THEIR FEET, SO THEY CAN TELL WHEN THEY LAND IF FOOD IS GOOD.

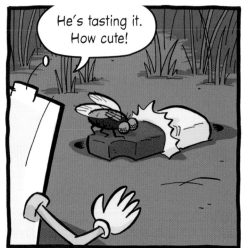

FLY spitting

FLIES USE SPIT TO TURN THEIR FOOD INTO LIQUID, THEN THEY SUCK IT UP AGAIN.

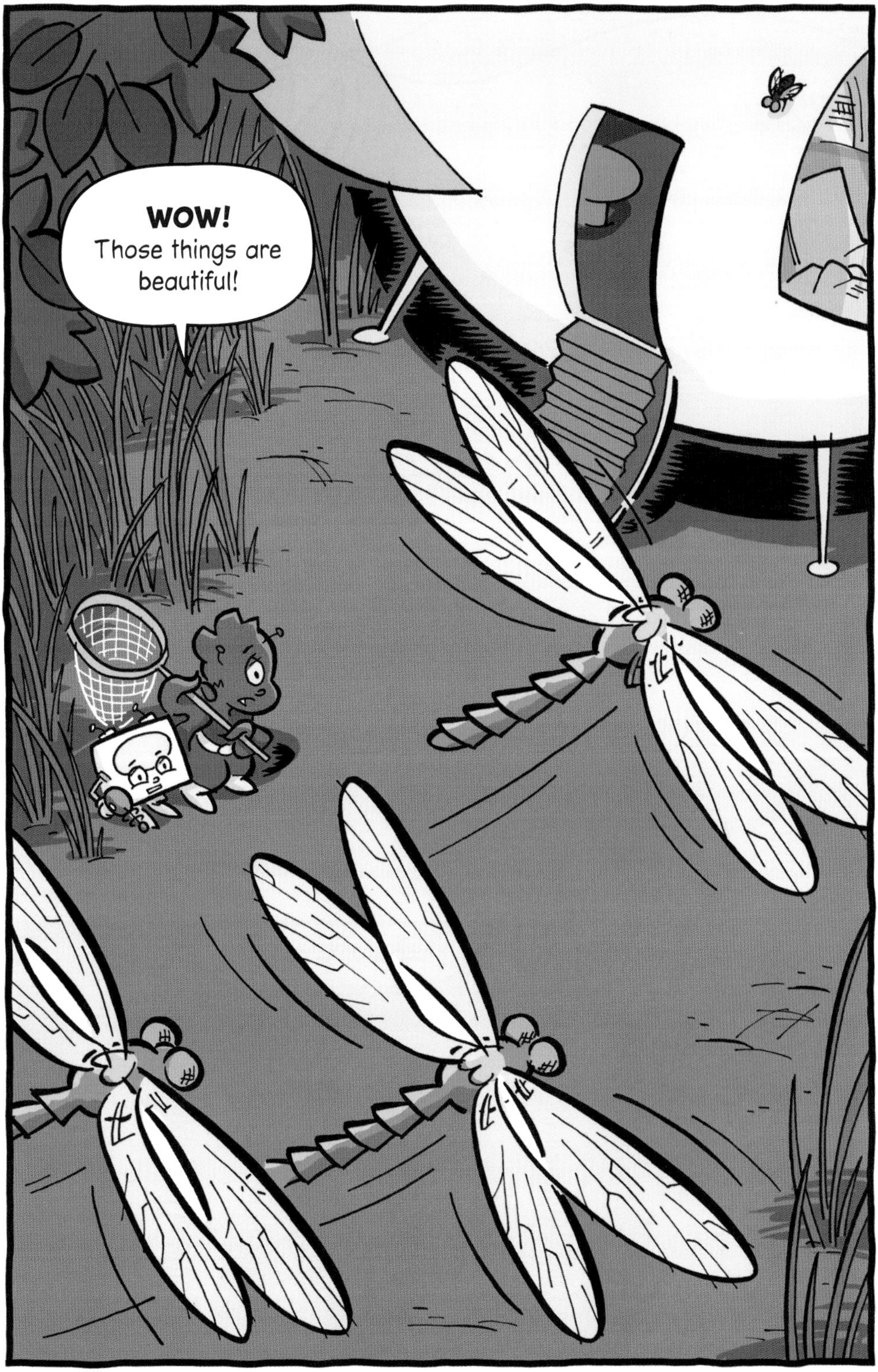
WOW!
Those things are beautiful!

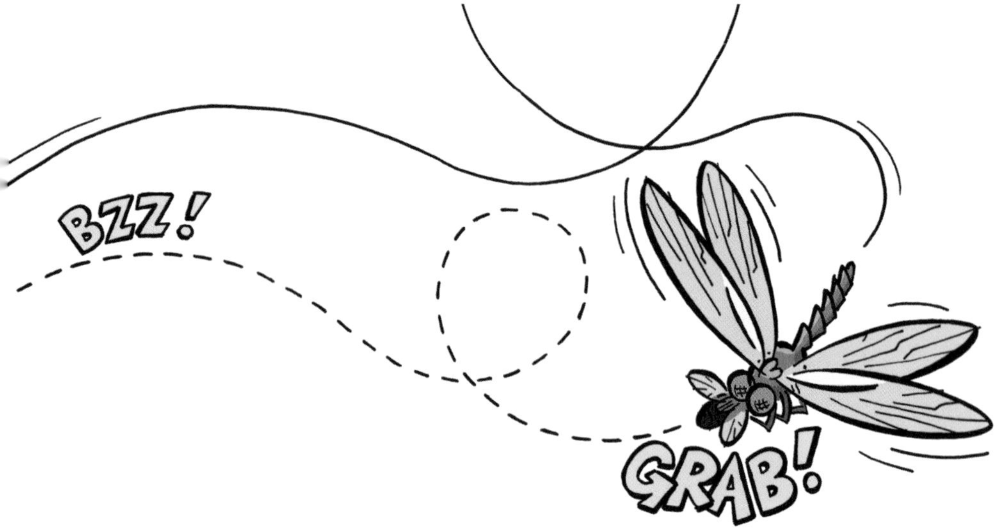
BZZ!
GRAB!

DRAGONFLY

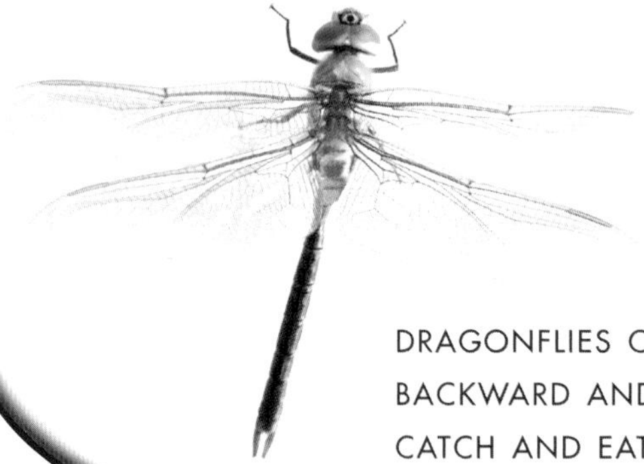

DRAGONFLIES CAN FLY FORWARD, BACKWARD AND SIDEWAYS. THEY CAN CATCH AND EAT PREY AS THEY FLY.

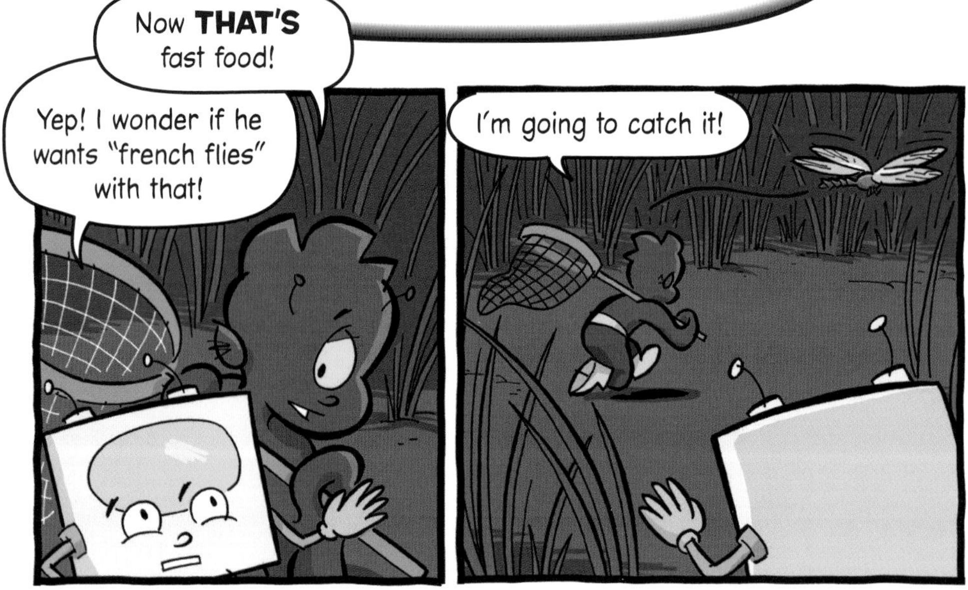
Now **THAT'S** fast food!
Yep! I wonder if he wants "french flies" with that!
I'm going to catch it!

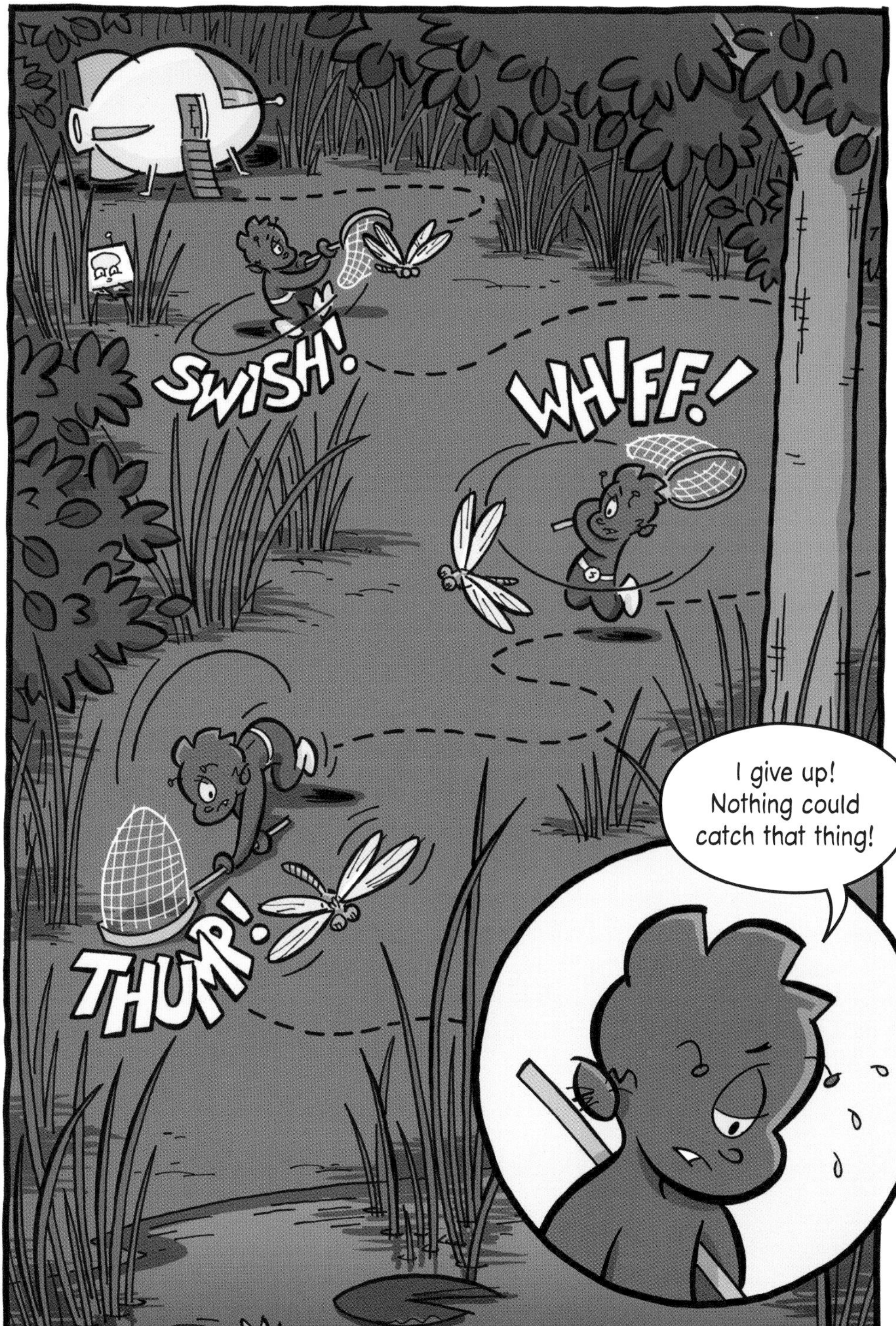
SWISH!
WHIFF!
THUMP!
I give up!
Nothing could
catch that thing!

It must be lunchtime around here.

Wow! This slimy green monster is the **PERFECT PET**, Zig.

FROG croaking

MALE FROGS CROAK TO PROTECT THEIR HOMES AND TO CALL TO LADY FROGS.

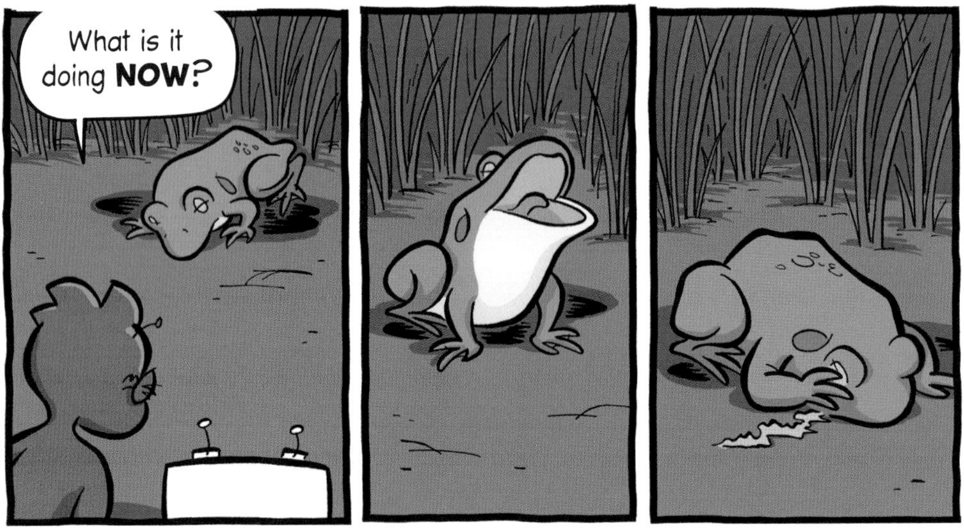
What is it doing NOW?

FROG eating its skin

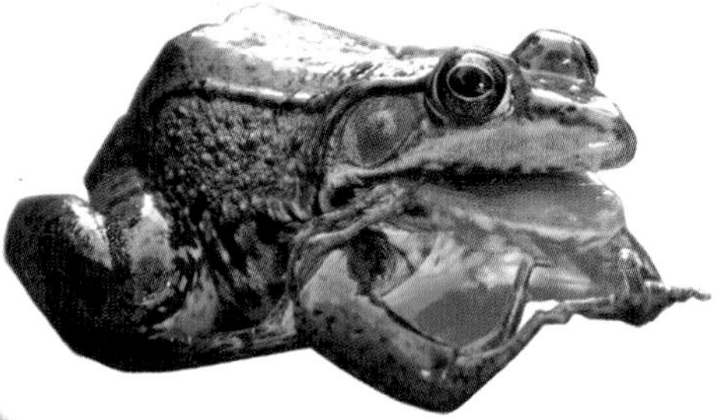

SOME FROGS SHED THEIR SKIN ABOUT ONCE A WEEK. AND THEN THEY EAT IT.

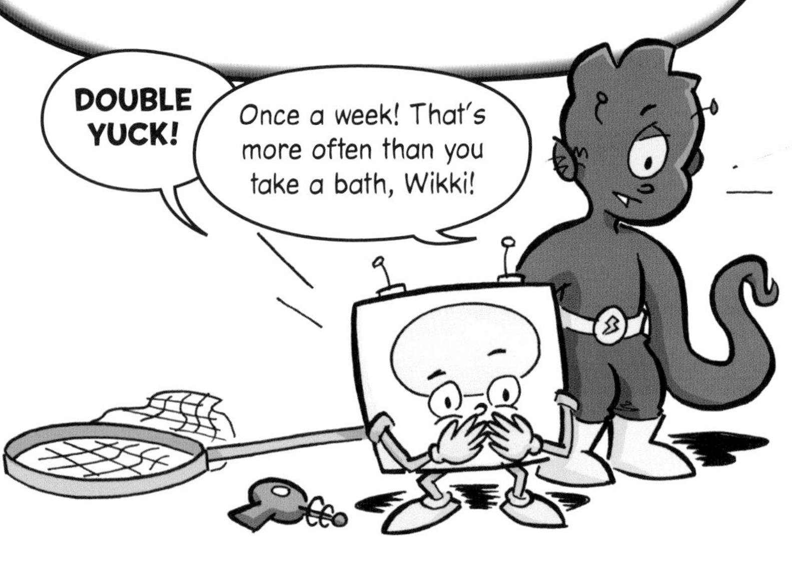
DOUBLE YUCK!
Once a week! That's more often than you take a bath, Wikki!

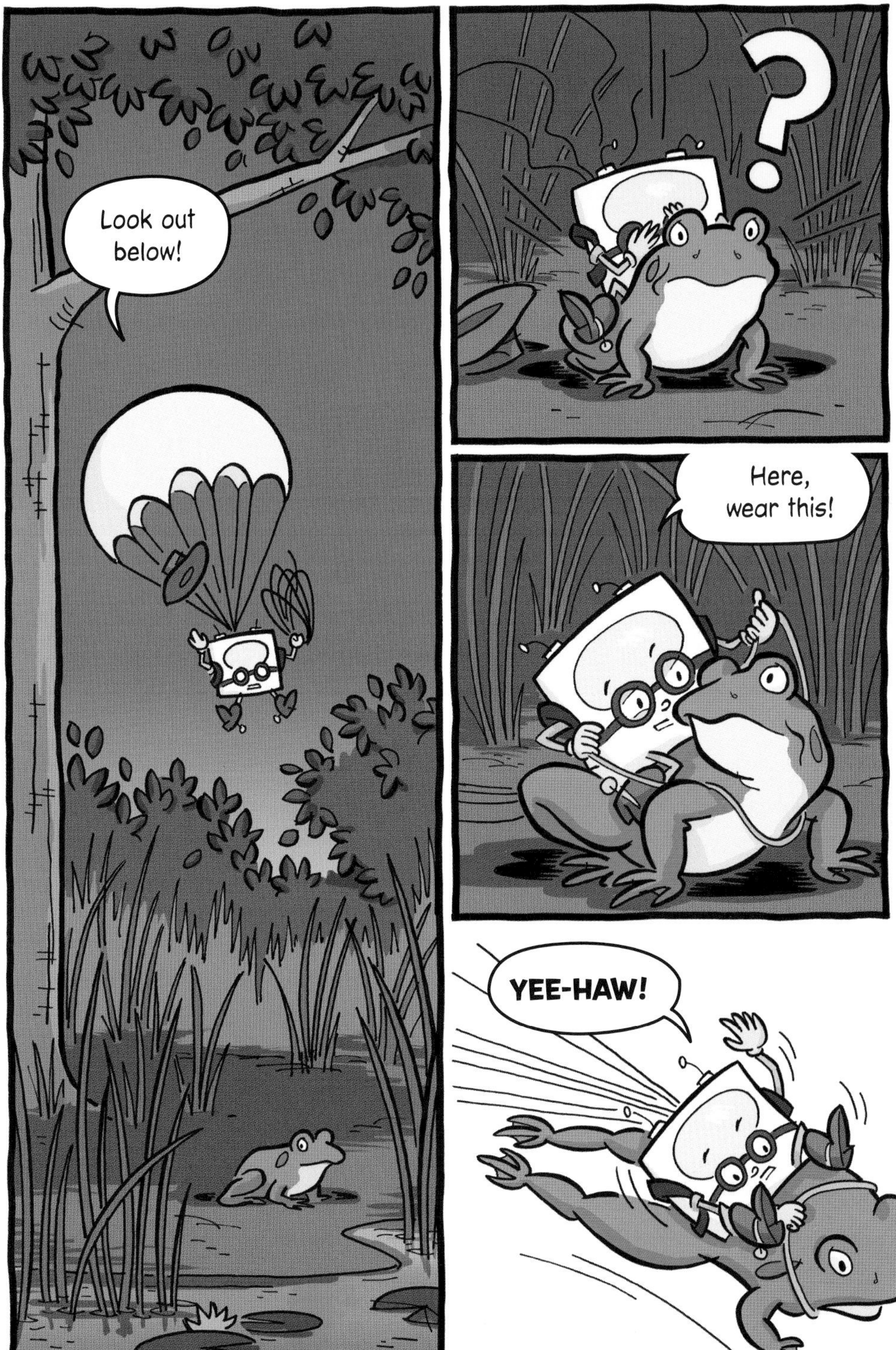
Look out below!
?
Here, wear this!
YEE-HAW!

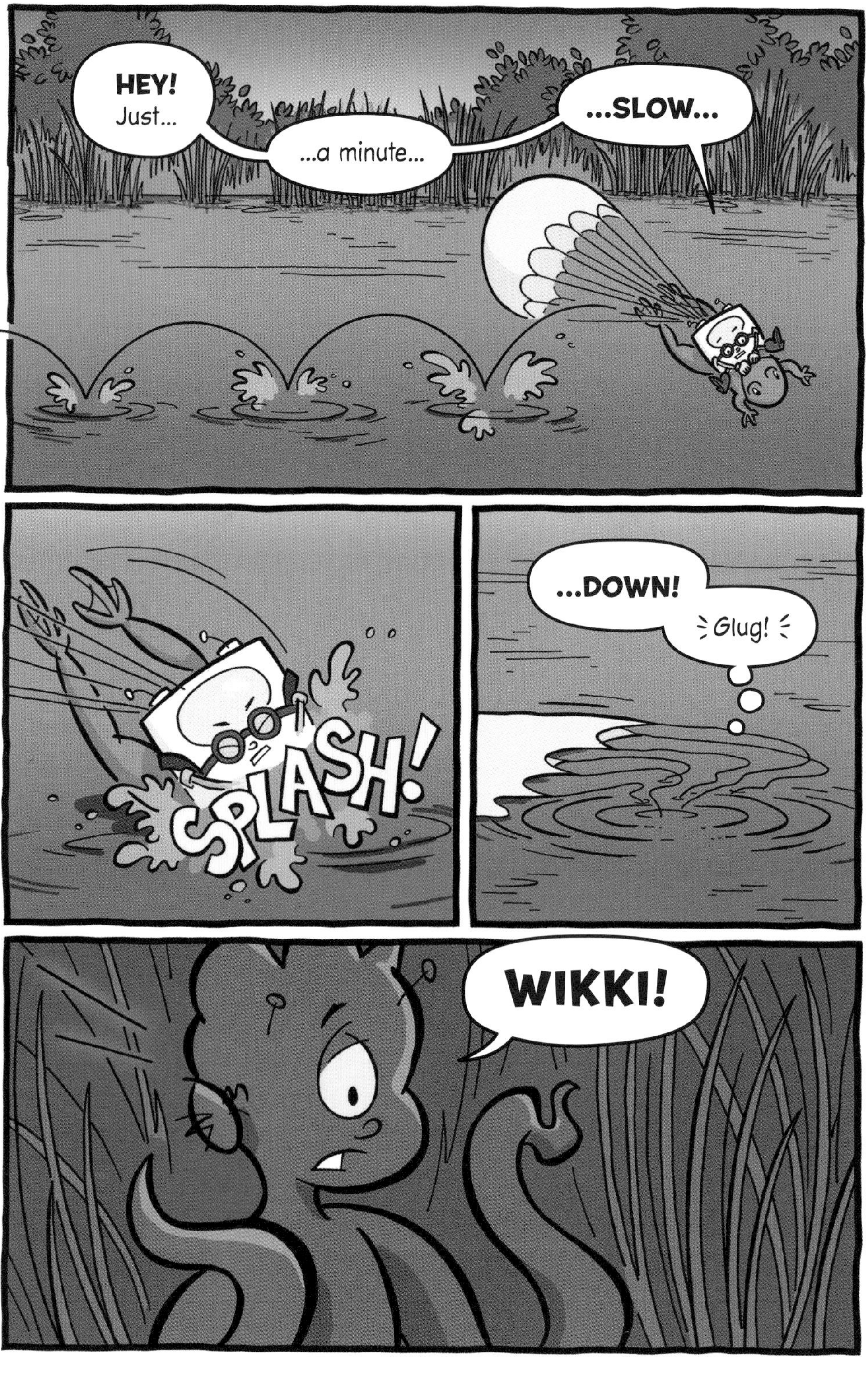
HEY! Just...
...a minute...
...SLOW...
SPLASH!
...DOWN!
Glug!
WIKKI!

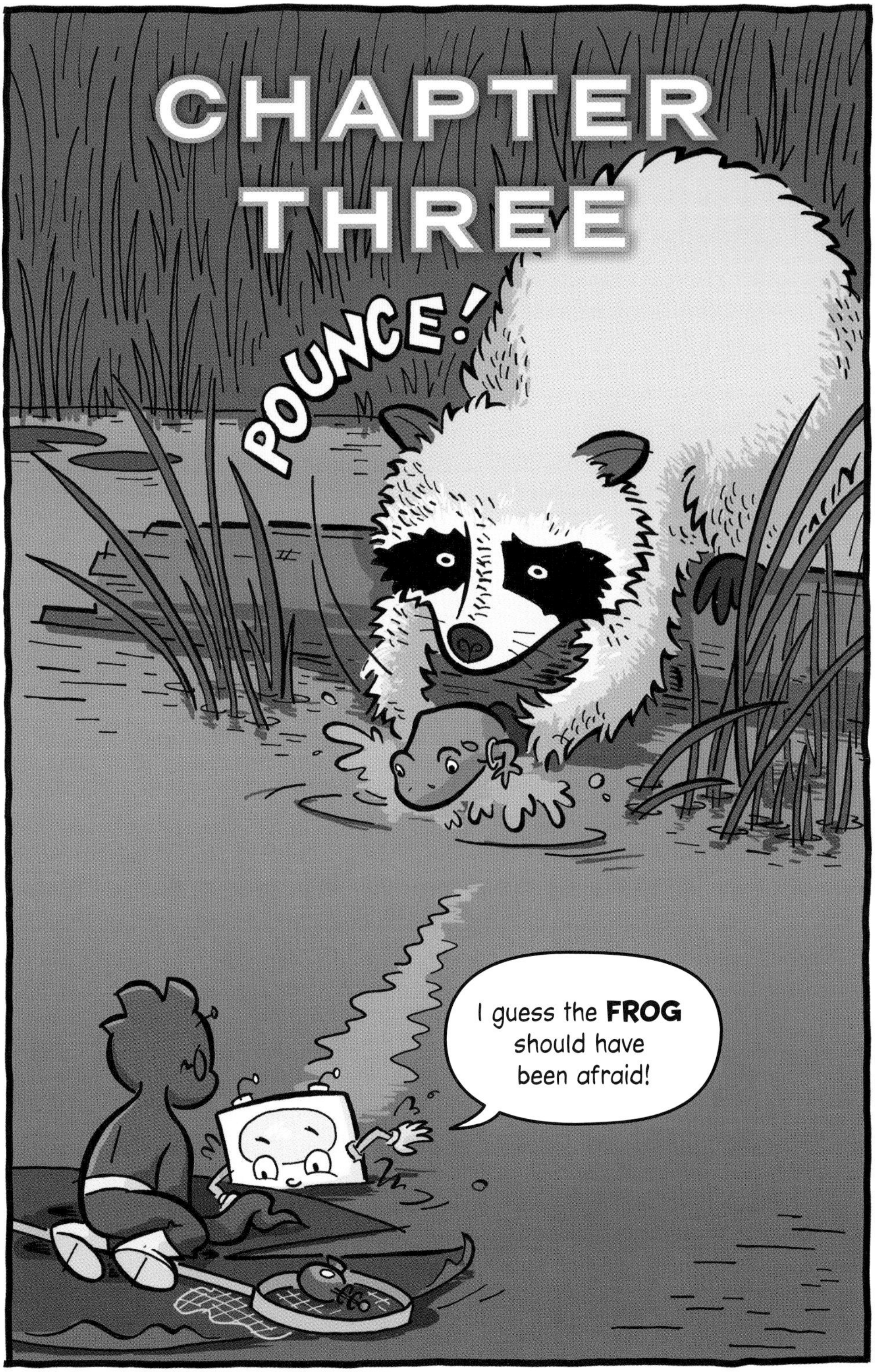
CHAPTER THREE
POUNCE!
I guess the **FROG** should have been afraid!

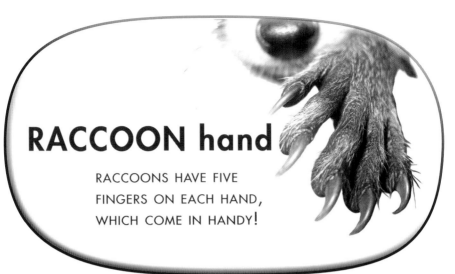

RACCOON hand

RACCOONS HAVE FIVE FINGERS ON EACH HAND, WHICH COME IN HANDY!

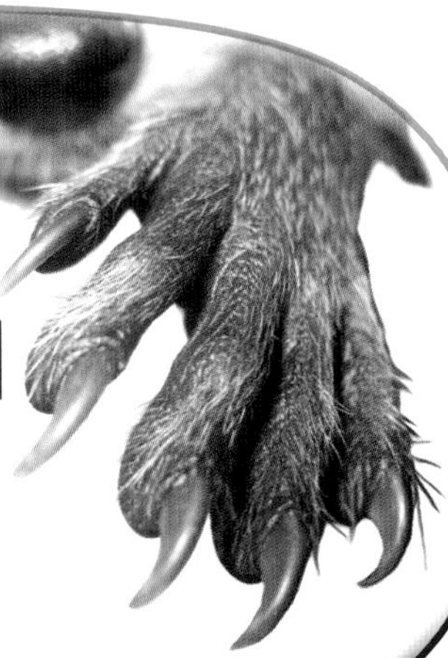

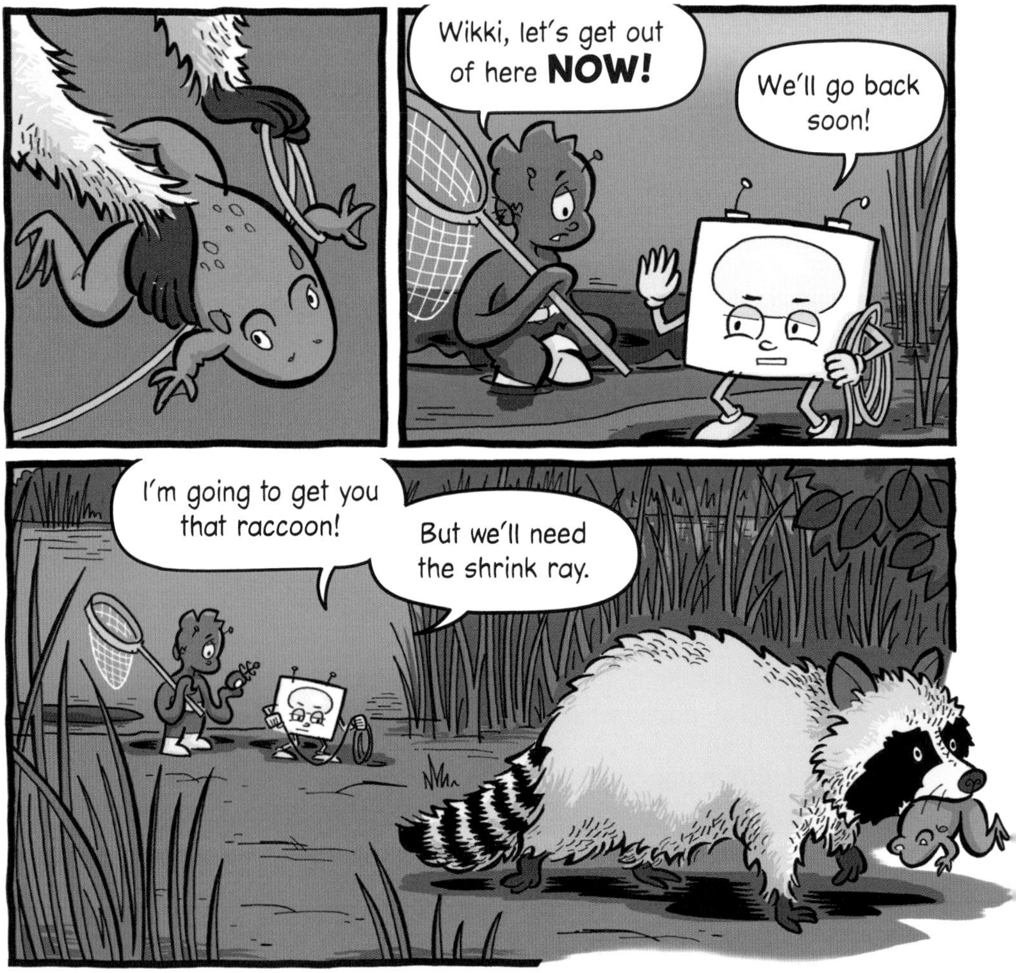

Wikki, let's get out of here **NOW!**
We'll go back soon!
I'm going to get you that raccoon!
But we'll need the shrink ray.

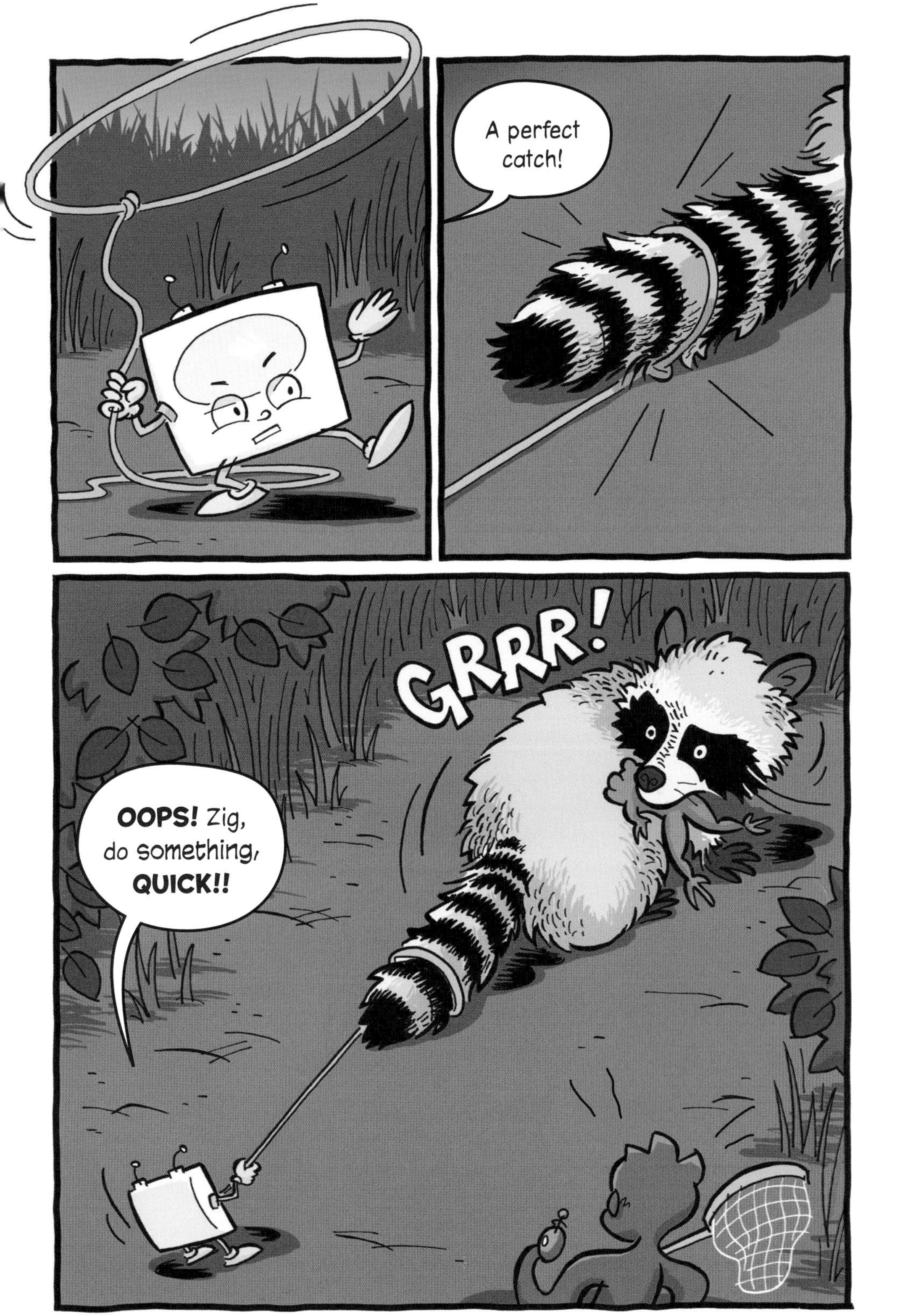
A perfect catch!
GRRR!
OOPS! Zig, do something, QUICK!!

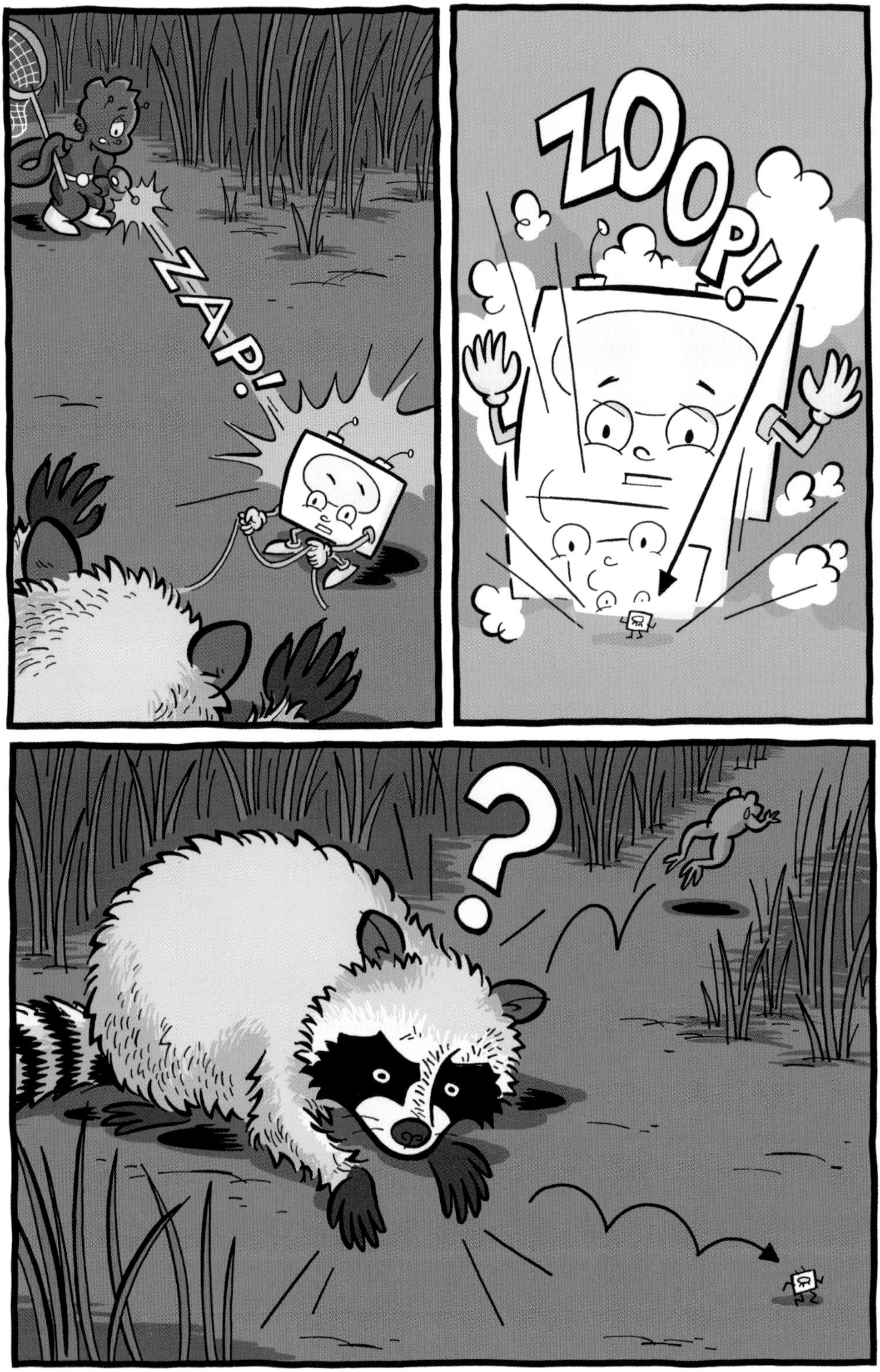
ZAP!
ZOOP!
?

Why didn't you zap the RACCOON!

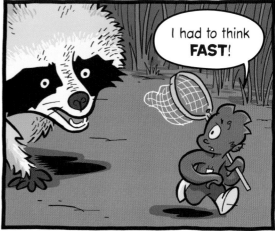

I had to think **FAST**!

That thing nearly ate **YOU** for lunch!

And the ship is about to **TAKE OFF!**

OOPS!

Ow!

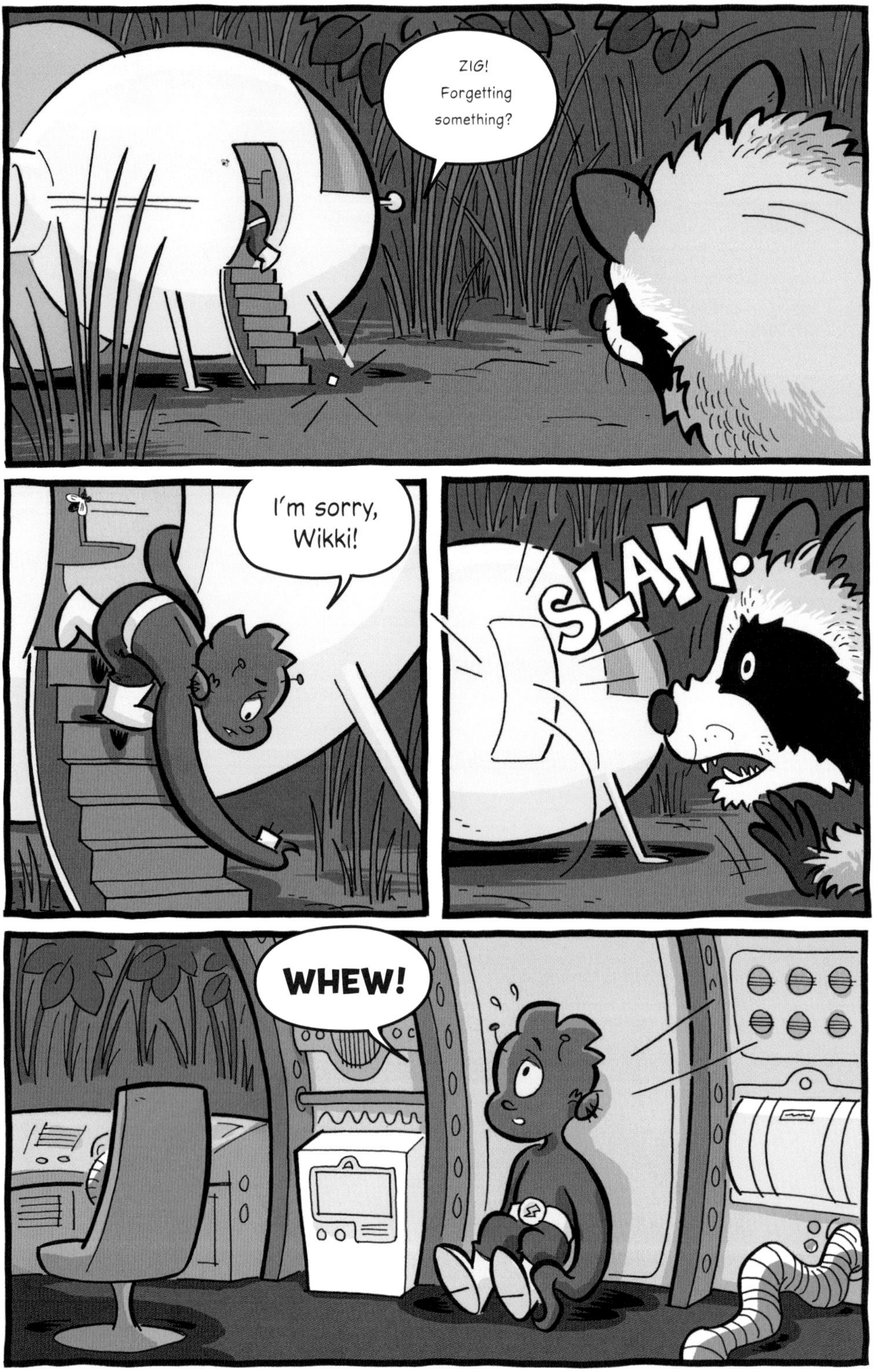
ZIG! Forgetting something?
I'm sorry, Wikki!
SLAM!
WHEW!

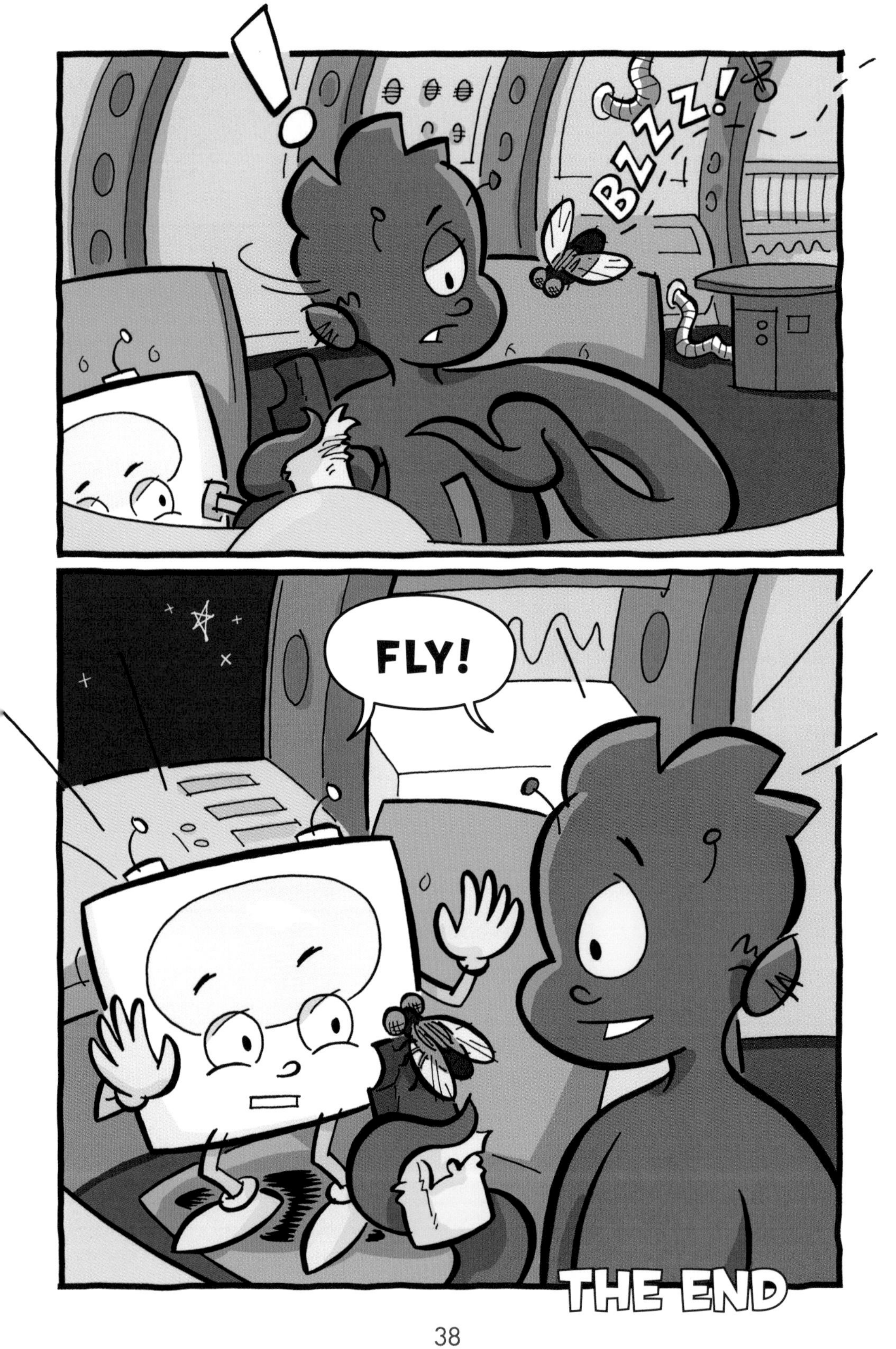
!
BZZZ!
FLY!
THE END

ABOUT THE AUTHORS

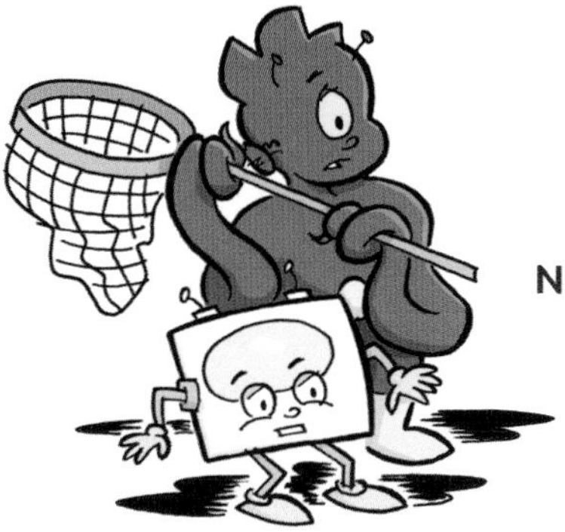

NADJA SPIEGELMAN, who wrote Zig and Wikki's story, recently graduated from Yale University as an English major. She grew up in New York City where there are few dragonflies and frogs, although there are certainly plenty of houseflies. When she was younger, she loved going to the country, where she collected insects and salamanders and kept them inside her shoe-box "bug museum." This is her first book.

TRADE LOEFFLER, who drew Zig and Wikki, grew up in Livermore, California. Unlike Zig and Wikki, he doesn't believe flies make good pets. But he did like to collect them when he was a kid—to feed them to the funnel spiders that lived in a field near his house. Trade now lives in New York City with his wife, Annalisa; son, Clark; and dog, Boo. He is the creator of the all-ages web comic *Zip and Li'l Bit* but this TOON book is Trade's first-ever work in print.

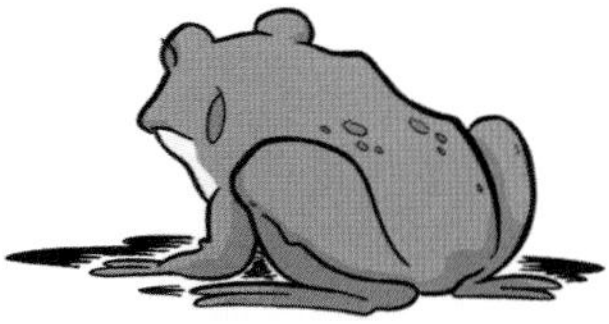

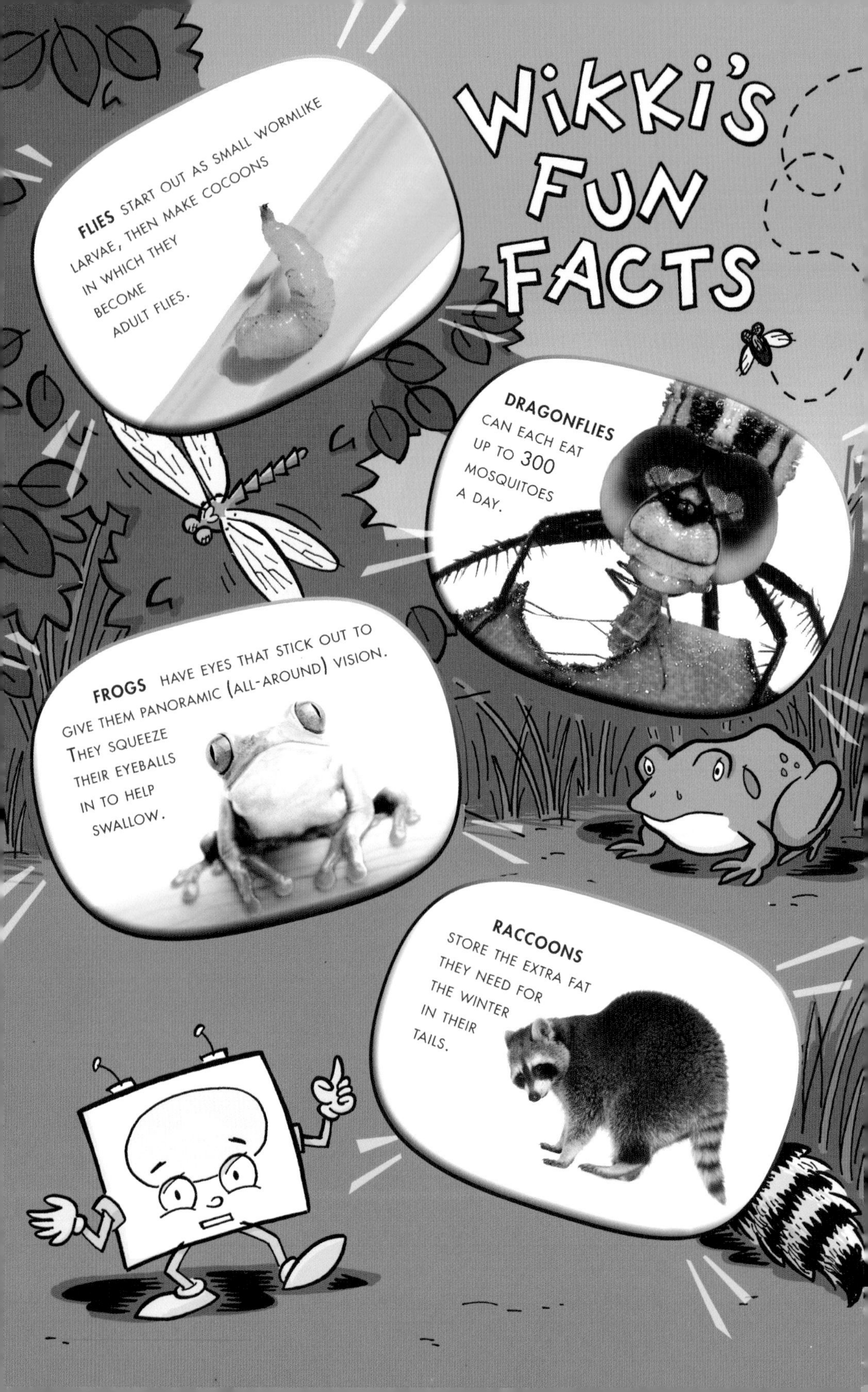

WIKKI'S FUN FACTS
FLIES START OUT AS SMALL WORMLIKE LARVAE, THEN MAKE COCOONS IN WHICH THEY BECOME ADULT FLIES.
DRAGONFLIES CAN EACH EAT UP TO 300 MOSQUITOES A DAY.
FROGS HAVE EYES THAT STICK OUT TO GIVE THEM PANORAMIC (ALL-AROUND) VISION. THEY SQUEEZE THEIR EYEBALLS IN TO HELP SWALLOW.
RACCOONS STORE THE EXTRA FAT THEY NEED FOR THE WINTER IN THEIR TAILS.